Salty Splashes

COLLECTION™

MOVIES ON PAPER

www.saltysplashes.com

Salty Splashes
COLLECTION™
MOVIES ON PAPER

Channel Blue

RIDERS OF THE STORM

JZ Bingham

Illustrations by Jason Buhagiar

BALCONY7
Media and Publishing
SANTA BARBARA, CALIFORNIA

Published by Balcony 7 Media and Publishing
133 East De La Guerra St., #177
Santa Barbara, CA 93101
(805) 679-1821
www.balcony7.com

ISBN: 978-1-939454-07-2
LCCN: 2013951029

Book Design and Production: Jason Buhagiar
Cover and Jacket Design and Illustrations: Jason Buhagiar
Art Direction: Balcony 7 Studios

Other Books In The Salty Splashes Collection

Dreamy Drums, Trouble in Paradise
Isle of Mystery, Eyes of the King
Gansevort, The King and His Court

Available As:
Jacketed Hardcovers
Read-To-Me eBooks
Regular eBooks
Trilogy Audiobook

Find them at major retailers, both online and physical,
and in public libraries across the United States and Canada.

Learn More By Visiting
www.saltysplashes.com

Follow Us On
Facebook - Twitter - Pinterest

The grass felt cool as Crump stretched out. He cried, "What a haul!"

Stump grinned and added, "Yeah! I guess you'd say we hit a wall!"

They laughed and stared up at the sky. Crump sighed. "Now ain't this nice?"

Stump smiled a while and chuckled. "Like a slice of Paradise!"

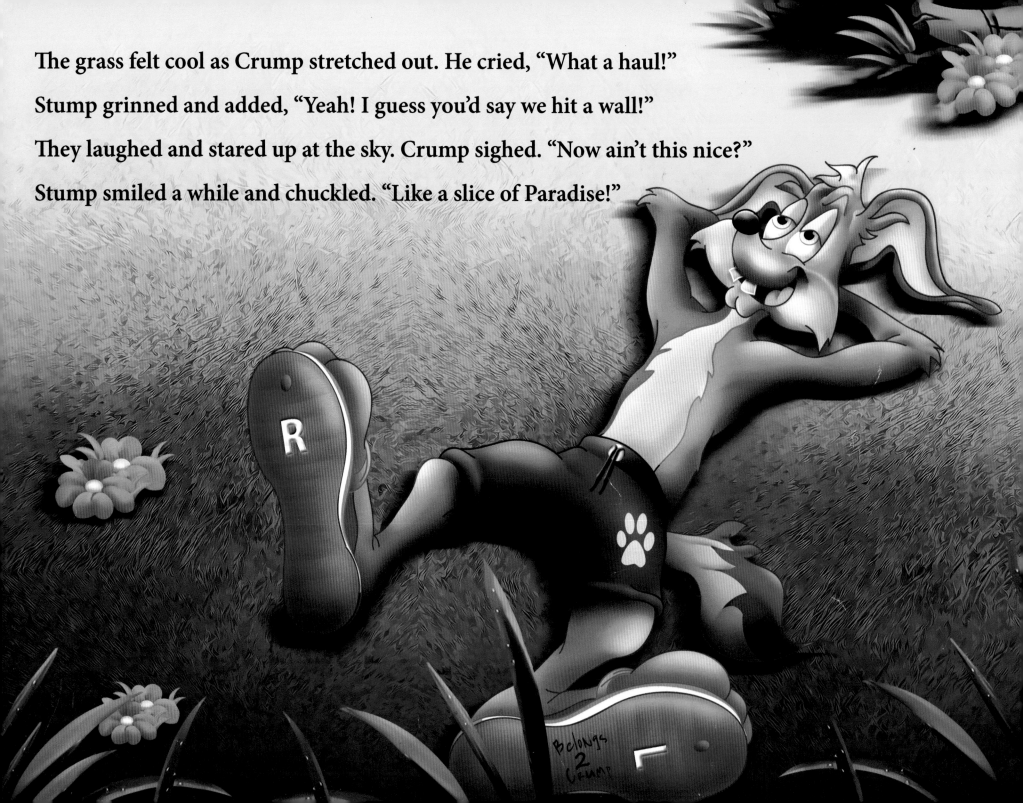

"You think that did the trick? You think the Boss'll think we're slick?"

Stump answered, "Hey, I'll lick your shoes if Plan One doesn't stick!"

They lay there gazing at the sky and grinning wide with pride.

If luck were on their side, they'll soon be riding with the tide.

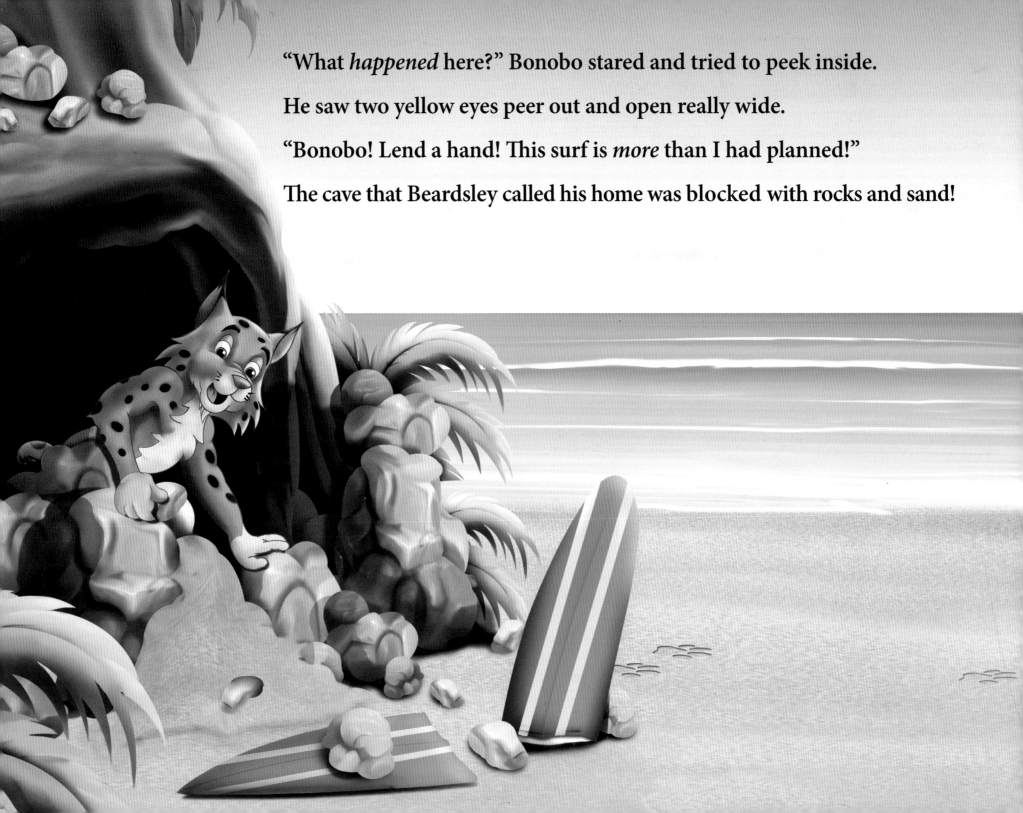

"What *happened* here?" Bonobo stared and tried to peek inside.

He saw two yellow eyes peer out and open really wide.

"Bonobo! Lend a hand! This surf is *more* than I had planned!"

The cave that Beardsley called his home was blocked with rocks and sand!

Bonobo set to work and moved enough to set him free.

When Beardsley squeezed out through the hole, guess what his eyes did see?

He saw his surfboard laying there. Its frame was split in two!

"It *wasn't* surf! It looks like someone's got it *in* for you!"

While walking down the path from Beardsley's cave to meet the gang,
Bonobo rolled his eyes and sighed. "Great! Here comes Yin and Yang!"

"Hey guys! What's happening? You heading over to the beach?"

Stump grinned these words with charming whiteness, full of overreach.

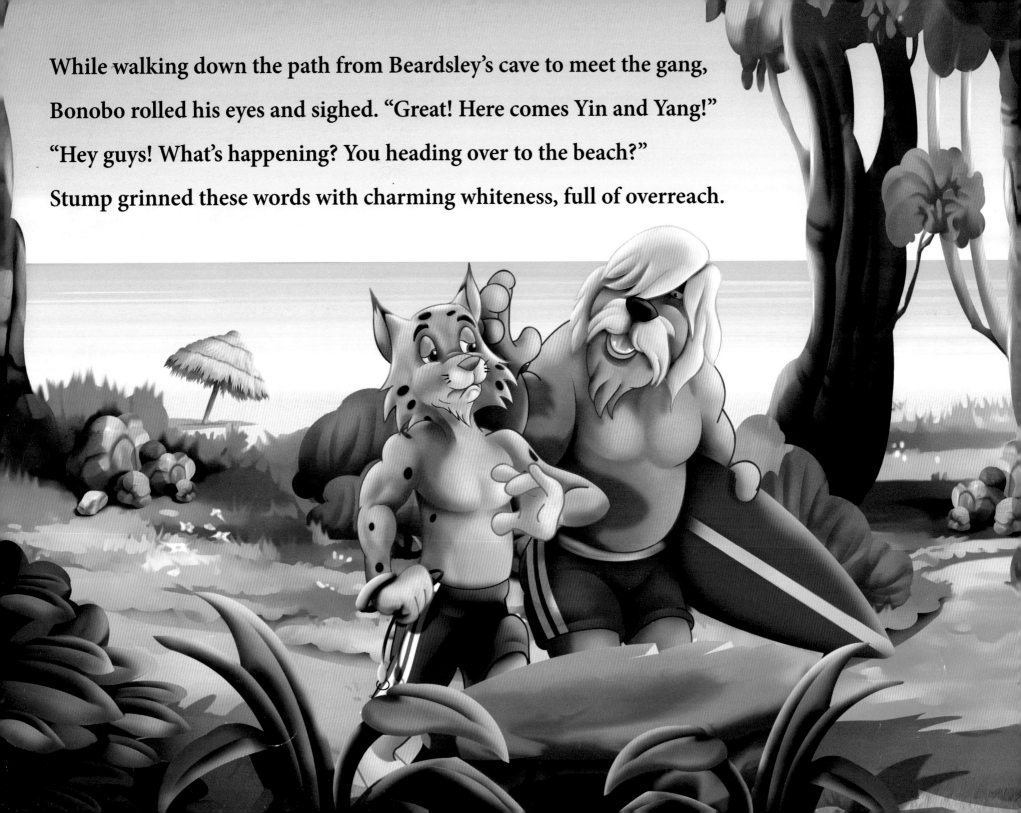

"Yeah, that we are! And how 'bout you? Where's Diggy and your crew?"

"Oh, they'll be waiting for us there. We had some things to do."

Bonobo winked at Beardsley, not believing this was true.

"What *else* is new? Let Diggy know, your work's cut out for you."

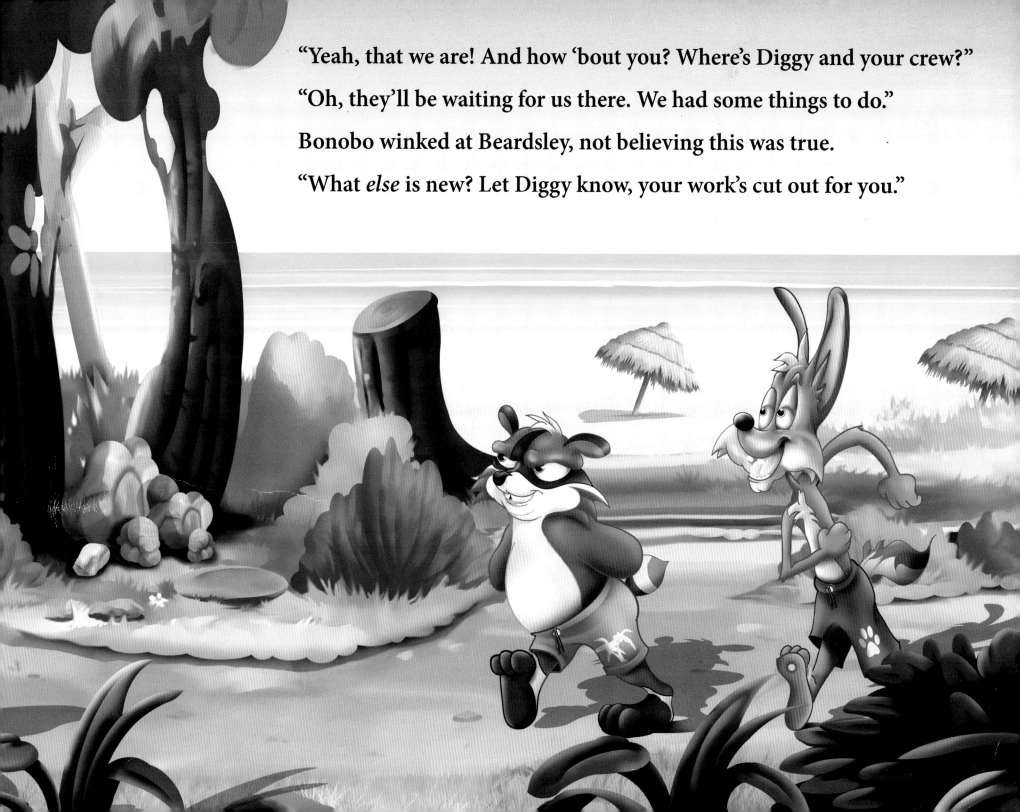

As Kat and Oola spread a heavy blanket in the sand,

they spotted Diggy strutting toward them showing off his tan.

"Well lookie here! This makes my year! The pretty musketeers!

And where's that newbie? What's his name? That cat with pointy ears!"

"Oh, *look* girls! It's Hot-*Diggity*! He's come to claim his prize!"

They laughed as Kat went on. "But *this* year, Beardsley's on the rise!"

"We'll find out soon enough. He ain't like me, so big and buff."

As Diggy said this, Kat sang out, "I bet he calls your bluff!"

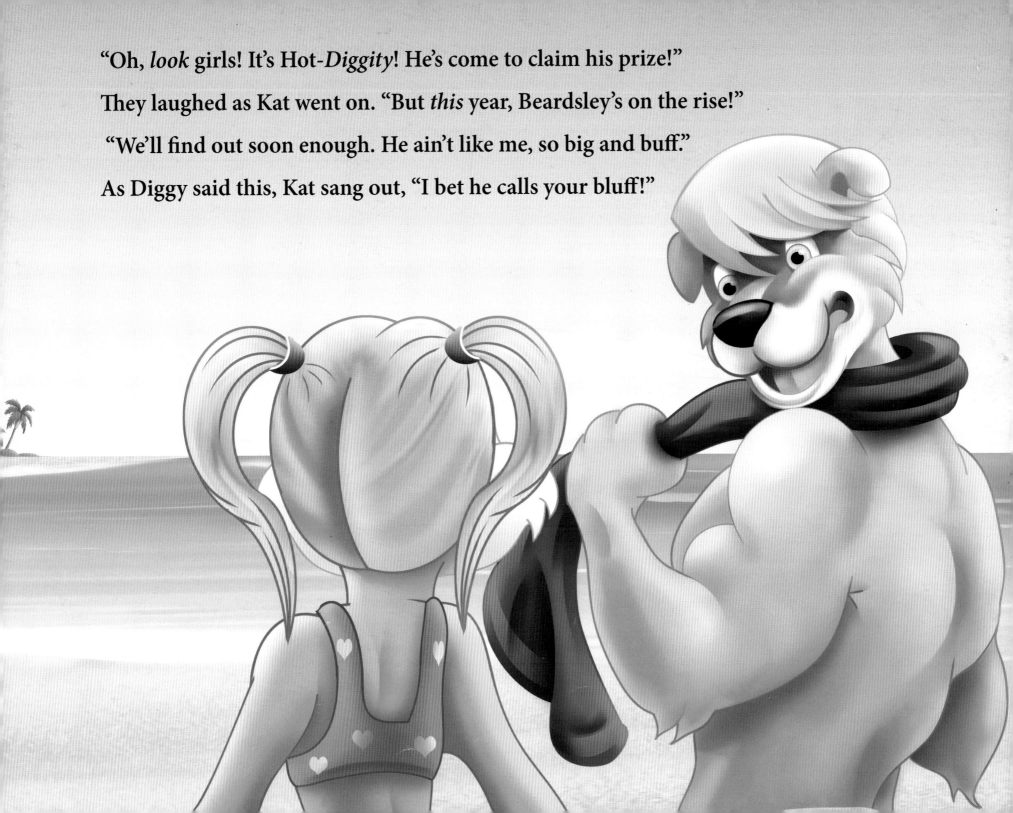

"What *happened* to your *board*?" Kat stared at Beardsley's mangled cord.

He nodded toward where Diggy lay. "They think they've got me *scored*.

But *now* I've got my eyes on them. No worries," Beardsley said.

"Each time they try to slow me down, I'll just *speed up* instead!"

Both Stump and Crump slumped down with thumps, prepared to take their lumps.

"I can't *believe* he got away! What are you, two big *chumps*?"

"We're *sorry* Boss! But we ain't through. We're working on Plan Two!"

But Stump's excuse was just no use. "Let's *hope*, or else you're *through*!"

Bonobo stood up in the sand, deciding to be bold.

"Here, take my board. It's been restored. Don't let him take the gold!"

"No way!" said Beardsley instantly, though touched by this display.

"I mean it!" said his friend quickly. "Go blow this dude away!"

While Beardsley bolted toward the surf to practice for the Heat,
the girls put on their snorkels, slipping fins onto their feet.
The foaming curls, like frosting swirls, were luring surfers out
while others swam beneath the waves to watch the fish and scout.

With surfers dashing through the thrashing splash of crashing swells,

the girls were gliding through the rising tide toward fish and shells.

The colors swimming all around, like rainbows soaked in brine,

delighted them with their displays of fins and teeth and spine!

As Kat swam up to get some air, she spied the puny pair

of Stump and Crump as off they swam toward some no-good affair.

She dove back under, toward the magic wonder of the blue.

Through muted thunder, waves did plunder stalks of kelp in two.

As hours did slide, the surf soon died, replaced with tide so high.

Back on the beach, the surfers took a break to rest and dry.

The bonfires started flickering with lights of gold and smoke.

The barbecues were sizzling with logs of burning oak.

Some groovy music, growing bright, replaced the dying sun.

The gnarly vibes would fill the night with dance and lots of fun!

The festive stage was all the rage, lit up with lights so grand!

A hometown shout was rockin' out from Curly Crush's band!

Far from this dill, hard-pressed to will, three surfers took a spill.

They waded in. Here would begin, Plan Two: the dreaded Fin.

The Diggy crew had plans to brew with this, the evil shark;

to make up for their failed attempt to mess with Beardsley's spark.

I'm listening," growled the massive form that floated in the light.

"We need your speed and all your steeds to help us win this fight!"

While Diggy talked, the shark did balk, but soon his eyes could see

the honor in defending his blue kingdom of the sea.

A crowd began to gather 'round to watch the Heat begin.

They soon would learn which one would earn the famous Golden Fin!

Their boards were tied to dolphin guides that pulled them like a sleigh

to what they called The Channel, every surfer's Dream Highway!

As, one by one, they took a run, the barrels quickly grew.

With every round the waves would crown with energy anew!

From on the shore, the crowd would roar whenever someone flew!

To win this game you'd have to tame the mighty Channel Blue!

The dolphins pulling Diggy's board rode into Beardsley's lane.

They bumped his board, not once, but twice. But ne'er did he complain!

"Nice try!" he yelled. These Diggy-tricks would seem to be in vain,

for Beardsley's will to win steamed like a locomotive train!

As Diggy blasted past him pulling off some showboat moves,

he shouted out, "Hot *dog,* bobcat! You checkin' out my *grooves*?"

But, in a flash, did Beardsley dash in front and make him crash!

"Hey, *sorry* Dude! You *say* something? I'm taking out the *trash*!"

While Diggy climbed back on his board to try to save some face,

he hung back just a bit to watch his dolphins brace to race!

They motored down, without a sound, right under Beardsley's board;

then swam back up, with great build-up, to knock him from his cord!

As Beardsley felt the swell of water rising under him,

he hung on tight with all his might preparing for a swim!

But bobcats have some major claws and his were digging in!

With all four paws, he drew some *"Awes!"* with catapulted spin!

Now quite enthused, he turned to choose when next to take his cue.

His eyes then spied a *monster wave* just coming into view!

With senses drawn, he focused on this *wicked wall of blue*.

His eyes grew wide. This rising tide was *too big to be true!*

His surfboard seemed to soar from underneath his gripping paws.

He held on fast and, like a mast, his board defied all laws!

While upside down, still spinning 'round, he braced to face his fall!

He sensed commotion under him: *a shark-infested brawl!*

While still up high, he heard the cry of dolphin squeals unite.

While falling down, he heard a sound of thunder-rolling might!

A whale was breaching under him, its tail just within sight!

Its motion broke his free-fall, saving him from quite a fright!

It was a sight to see, this big, blue beast of majesty!

As it held court, all breath cut short to watch him part the sea!

His surfboard dropped with grace atop a freshly molded wave.

It curled away from all the fray; *an epic, winning save*!

The crowd looked on with faces drawn, not knowing what to think.

They saw two surfers rise and sink in just one fleeting blink!

Then, suddenly, their eyes did see the groovy mastery

of Beardsley riding toward them on a wave of victory!

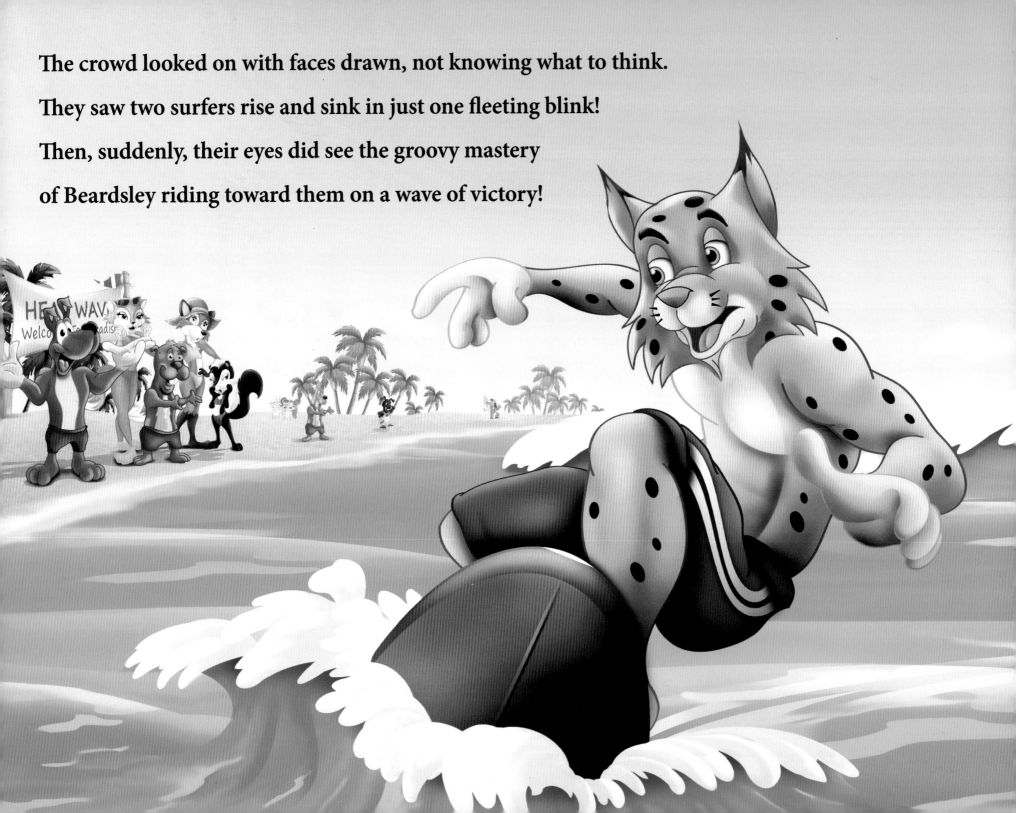

"One down," they thought. "One more to go." They scouted high and low
to catch a glimpse of Diggy's board, expecting him to show.
A hush of worry settled in, until they saw the fin
of Diggy's board and then his cord and then his sheepish grin.

Amidst the cheers of all their peers, the band began to play.

The win this year, it seemed real clear, was Beardsley's all the way!

With Diggy looking down-and-out and brushing off the sand,

did Beardsley find him through the crowd and offer him his hand.

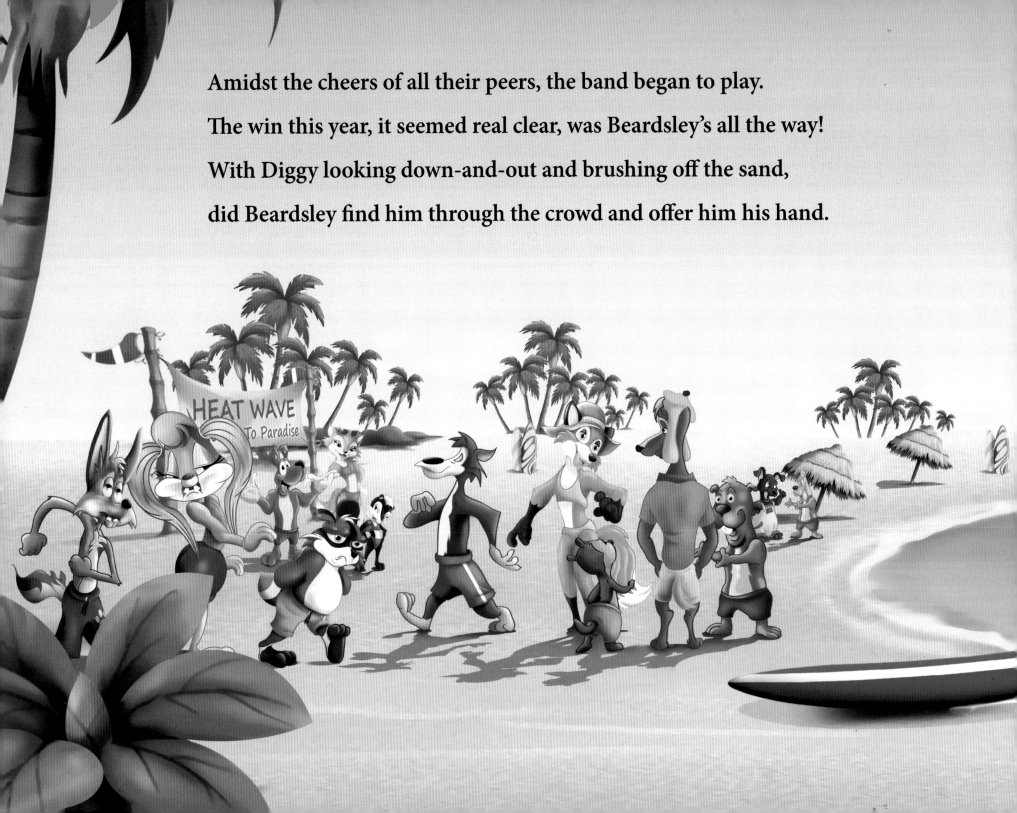

In spite of all his scheming and in spite of all his tricks,

the mighty Diggy hit a wall with quite a lot of bricks.

"We made it, man. Here, take my hand." The bobcat took a stand.

This humbled Diggy mightily. He grinned and took his hand.

The Golden Fin was quite a sight: a trophy, big and bright.

A symbol of a surfer battling the ocean's might.

As friends and fans made good on plans to dance and prance and play,

the sun would soon be fading fast to chase another day.

While stepping back to grab a snack, the girls did spy the pair

of Beardsley and his newfound friend walk off without a care.

Kat noticed Diggy laughing while they headed toward the sun.

As Beardsley nudged him lightly, she could see they *both* had won.

THE END

MOVIES ON PAPER

www.saltysplashes.com

Salty Splashes

COLLECTION™

MOVIES ON PAPER

www.saltysplashes.com